THE O~

G~

BOOK IV

STARS

OF

OLYMPUSS

ROBIN PRICE

THE FELINE
EMPIRE

MOUNT
OLYMPUSS

TRAY

THE SQUEAK ISLANDS

MISR
(FLEAGYPT)

THE OLYMPUSS GAMES

BOOK IV: STARS OF OLYMPUSS

First published by Mogzilla in 2016
Paperback edition:
ISBN: 9781906132842

Printed in the UK

The Olympuss Games

BOOK I Son of Spartapuss   ISBN: 9781906132811

BOOK II Eye of the Cyclaw   ISBN: 9781906132835

BOOK III Maze of the Minopaw ISBN: 9781906132828

BOOK IV Stars of Olympuss   ISBN: 9781906132842

www.mogzilla.co.uk/shop

WWW.SPARTAPUSS.CO.UK

THE STORY SO FAR...

The OLYMPUSS GAMES series is set in ancient Rome where cats rule the world and people have never existed.

The first book in the series is called: SON OF SPARTAPUSS.

SON OF SPARTAPUSS (or 'S.O.S.' for short) is a young ginger cat from the Land of the Kitons (Britain). He has just moved to Rome with his mother.

At the market he meets FURIA, a mysterious cat with orange eyes. S.O.S. buys FURIA at the auction, but she is far more expensive than he thinks. When S.O.S. can't pay, the seller calls the guards. S.O.S. is fined ten silver coins. An old cat called FATHER FELINIOUS offers to pay the fine if S.O.S. joins his gladiator school: THE SCHOOL FOR STRAYS. When he learns that FELINIOUS is FURIA's new owner, S.O.S. agrees to go. FURIA escapes from the school but gets caught. PUSSPERO MAXI, FURIA and S.O.S. fight their first gladiator battle together. Furia defeats a giant from Cattage.

The second book in the series is called: EYE OF THE CYCLAW.

Excitement spreads around the SCHOOL FOR STRAYS when an official arrives and asks the school to send athletes to take part in the famous GAMES.

Meanwhile, we learn that the mysterious FURIA is on a quest to recover four STRAYBOS (charms that are hidden in different places around the FELINE EMPIRE). She has one already and the second STRAYBO is hidden somewhere in the SCHOOL FOR STRAYS. MAXI and the SON OF SPARTAPUSS join FURIA on her quest to find the other missing charms. A clue suggests that one straybo has been hidden near MOUNT OLYMPUSS, where the GAMES are about to be held. The third book in the series is called: MAZE OF THE MINOPAW. In this book our heroes get shipwrecked on the island of Knossos and come face to face with mean KING MINOS and his mythical maze. Once the third straybo is recovered, they set sail for Mount Olympuss, where the games are about to begin, and the fourth and final straybo can be found.

THE SECRET DIARY OF S.O.S.

MEWNONIUS XXIX

June 30th

Dear mother, I expect you have been wondering what happened to me since I sent my last scroll. Well, I made it to Mount Olympuss for the games. I took a nasty bang on the head during my first boxing match and I'm afraid I can't remember anything that happened. Luckily one of my friends has finished off this diary so you can hear the end of the tale. I have to warn you that this time I got into a lot of trouble with skelton warriors, a three-headed dog called Furrburus and a snake-headed monster who needed a hair cut! So please don't read this before you take your afternoon cat nap or you might have nightmares.

Your son.

P.S. I promise to clean my room when I get back.

The Games Can Wait

Maxi and I wanted to set off for the Olympuss games as soon as our ship arrived in port. But our master, Felinious had other ideas.

"The road for Olympuss is far too dangerous at night," he warned.

Maxi's tail started to flick. He had a pained look on his face, like a dog that had just had its favourite bone taken away.

"We can look after ourselves," Maxi insisted. "We're gladiators, remember?"

Felinous stopped grooming his silver coat. He looked at the beam of Affleana, which Maxi held in his left paw. The old grey piece of wood was smoother than a pebble. It had been cut from a tree in one of Affleana's orchards. I waited, half expecting the legendary beam to speak... but it didn't.

"Come on," moaned Maxi. "What possible danger can we be in?"

"The closer you get to Mount Olympuss, the more powerful the beam will become," explained Felinious patiently.

"The more powerful it gets, the better," said Maxi. "The beam protects us."

Felinious flashed a dark look towards my impatient friend.

"I'll take good care of it, if that's what you're worried about," added Maxi.

"I'm not worried about the beam," he said. "I'm worried about the damage that you two could cause."

Outside, the seagulls were turning circles in the strong east wind. The ship swayed gently on the rising tide. Maxi let out a hiss of frustration and left Felinious in his cabin. I thought we were going to have to wait until morning for Felinious to fall asleep. Maxi and I waited patiently. Wave after wave of tiredness overtook the old cat until at last he set sail for dreamland.

"Is he REALLY asleep?" whispered Maxi. "Old Felinious is as sly as a Minopaw."

"Let's move," I whispered urgently. "Let's go now."

Our Olympuss adventure was about to begin. Maxi dropped a note that said: "See you at the games Felinious," under the old cat's paw. We crept out of the cabin like a couple of timid mice. As soon as we saw that the coast was clear, we took off like a pair of racing rats at the circus. On the deck of our ship *The Pawgo*, a gust of wind almost blew my fur off.

"For Peus sake!" I shivered. "I thought that the Squeak islands were supposed to be warm. It's freezing my whiskers off."

"Cheer up Spartan," smiled Maxi. "You are in the Port of Plaka. It is famous for its wind. It's windier than you are after you've scoffed three bowls of spicy chicken."

No one gets to choose their nickname. I HATE being called 'the Spartan'. My father got the name 'Spartapuss' because he used to work in a spa. It has nothing at all to do with Spartan warriors. I've explained this to Maxi a thousand times but he won't stop calling me 'Spartan'. This drives me mad but I decided to keep my mouth shut.

We padded down the gang plank of *The Pawgo* and away into the dark night. High in the cloudless sky I saw a cold slice of silver moon. The seagulls wheeled above us, calling like sirens.

I am good at getting into trouble. So no one was more surprised than me that we managed to make it out of the Port without any unexpected problems. There were no: angry pirates; shady sailors; crooked shop-keepers or evil slave-traders in sight.

The town of Plaka is built out of ancient stone. It is warm and golden during the daytime but it looked cold and blue in the moonlight.

We passed through the empty streets heading up the hill. At last we came to a white tower that stood taller than the mast of *The Pawgo*. Lamplight beckoned invitingly from a crack in the door.

"Good," said Maxi in excitement. "We are on the right path."

"What are those things?" I asked. I looked up at the carved figures on the side of the ghost-white tower.

"They're sundials," explained Maxi. "Shame they don't work in moonlight. This place is called *The Tower of the Wind*."

"I wonder why," I said with a shiver.

"WINDS!" called a voice from somewhere high above us.

"What was that you said Spartan?" asked Maxi.

"Nothing," I replied. "I didn't say anything."

Then I spotted it.

"Er... Maxi..." I whispered. "I think we'd better leave."

"Hang on a moment Spartan," he replied. "I just need to get my bearings. The North Star is over there somewhere..."

Leaning the bag containing the magic beam against the wall of the tower, Maxi gazed up into the inky black sky. But as soon as the bag touched the stone tower there was a spark of light. It was as if a red shooting star had dropped out of the sky and fallen into Maxis's bag. Maxi swung around in surprise and stood gaping.

"It's The Tower of The WINDS, not WIND!" boomed a voice as old as Mount Olympuss.

We looked on in amazement as one of the carvings near the window poked its marble face out of the wall. My jaw dropped as it started stroking its stony beard. There was a grinding noise as the stonework around its mouth shifted into a frown.

"There are four winds. Boreas and I are the main ones. The others are minor winds."

"Minor?" howled an angry voice.

A second figure had come alive. As quick as a whip, it drew a stone arrow from its quiver, strung the arrow into its bow and took aim.

"Who are you calling minor?" demanded the angry archer. "Take that back!"

"Steady Eurus!" said the first wind. "There's no need to start blowing hot."

I turned to Maxi.

"The bag with the beam!" I hissed.

"What's that Spartan?" replied Maxi, gawping at the stone archer in amazement.

"Grab the bag and run!" I ordered.

Maxi didn't need time to think. He grabbed the bag and took off like a chariot. Behind me, I heard a boom as Boreas, the North Wind joined in the fun. He was armed with thunderbolts.

We didn't stop running till we reached the city wall. I ran so fast that I thought that my heart would burst.

"What in the name of mighty Mewpiter was that all about?" asked Maxi.

"The beam," I gasped. "It started glowing. Then the carvings up on the tower suddenly... came to life."

Maxi scratched his ear.

"Felinious tried to warn us about this sort of thing, didn't he?" he said.

I nodded.

"The closer it gets to Mount Olympuss, the more powerful it gets," roared Maxi, doing a good impression of the booming voice of Felinious.

"We got away with it that time Spartan," laughed Maxi. "Let's crack on, you don't get crowned champion of Olympuss for sitting on the wall. Don't forget what we're here for..."

The Olympuss games. That's what we'd come here for. Or was it? Maxi seemed to have forgotten all about our friend Furia and her quest to find the missing 'straybos' – the hidden charms that she was collecting and wearing on her collar. We'd both promised to help Furia find the last missing charm. But the fever of the games had wiped all thoughts of our quest from Maxi's memory.

Fallen Leaf

It took us the best part of a day to make our way from the town to the Olympuss gate. As the day wore on we met more and more travellers on the road to Olympuss. It felt great to be part of something this big. These games are famous throughout the Feline Empire. Competitors come from Fleagypt and Cattage, from Hisspania and Purrmania, all bound for the glory of the games.

The sun was high in the sky as we joined the line at the gate where athletes were saying goodbye to their friends and family. Only athletes are allowed to pass through the gate of Peus into the village where the competitors live during the five days of the games.

"Excuse me!" mewed a tabby as he pushed his way through the crush. I have to say that he didn't look much like an athlete, unless he was taking part in a cream licking competition.

"Hey! Wait!" thundered Maxi. Maxi sprang after the stranger, shouting at him to stop. By the time I caught up with the them, I was relieved to see the stranger shaking paws with Maxi. The tabby was reattaching a silver leaf charm to his collar.

"Thank goodness you spotted it," gasped the stranger, looking relieved. "My silver leaf must have fallen off in the crush."

"It is valuable?" I asked.

"It is beyond price," said the tabby, proudly stroking the leaf. "This shows everyone that I'm taking part in the games."

"So are we!" said Maxi in excitement.

"We don't have silver leaves yet," I said.

The stranger gave Maxi a worried look.

"No silver leaves?" he said. "They won't

let you through the gate without them."

"Is there an Olympuss gift shop near here?" I asked.

"The silver leaves of the games are not for sale!" said the horrified tabby.

Maxi bashed me hard on the nose.

"Miaooowch!" I moaned.

"Excuse my Spartan friend's silly sense of humour. Of course the silver leaves are not for sale," said Maxi.

"Thanks again," said the tabby. I could tell by his flicking tail that he wanted to be on his way. Maxi looked like a wolf that had missed out on a free sheep dinner.

"Don't worry," I said, "I expect they will have a list at the gate. They are sure to be expecting us."

The Shouting Match

The louder Maxi spoke, the louder the guard shouted back. Maxi's fur was sticking out like a brush and his ears were back.

"Look – there's been some kind of mistake. We HAVE qualified for the games," insisted Maxi, for the third time.

"Really?" said the guard in the snooty

tone of a shop assistant in an expensive shop talking to a customer who'd asked the price of something he could not afford.

"Yes, REALLY!" insisted Maxi. "But we don't have our silver leaves with us..."

The guard's orange eyes went wide in mock surprise.

"Is that so?" he hissed.

"You have to let us in!" growled Maxi.

"He means that if you wouldn't mind just checking your list. We are sure that our names will be down on it," I added in my creamiest voice.

There was not a cat in the Underworld's chance that the guard was going to let us in. The crowd behind us was getting impatient. Some of them held up their silver leaves and began to push past us. A huge cat padded up and stood within a whisker of Maxi's face.

"Hey Romans – no silver leaf, no entry! Now get out of the way," he growled.

But Maxi was not going anywhere.

"Hey friend," Maxi said to the newcomer. "I see you've got a silver leaf. As a fellow competitor, you'll understand our situation."

The white cat didn't look very understanding.

"What sport is it that you do?" asked Maxi, "Flea picking?"

The white cat drew himself up to his full height and extended his claws. He was bigger than Maxi.

"Boxing." he growled.

"Boxing?" laughed Maxi. "Really? You surprise me. What a coincidence! Me too? How about if I challenged you to a boxing match? Would you..."

I should have seen it coming. The white cat's yellow eyes had been smouldering all through Maxi's speech. His tail had been thumping against the ground sending great clouds of dust up into the air. Without warning, his paw shot towards Maxi's face and caught him hard on the nose. Maxi wobbled and crashed down like a felled tree. The white cat stood over Maxi, looking pleased with his morning's work.

"That went well," I whispered.

Maxi struggled to get up from the dust.

"Shut up Spartan!" he hissed, getting to his feet. "I'd like to see you do better."

Before Maxi got up, the white cat

snatched a spear and lunged. Maxi had the sense to roll out of the way but the blow glanced his tail. More guards had joined us at the gate. They stood in a tight circle around Maxi. I stepped forward, determined to help my friend, but I felt a paw on my shoulder.

"Hold it!" called a voice.

The white cat was big, but the stranger at my side loomed up behind me like a mountain of fur.

"Put down the spear," said the stranger in a voice used to giving commands.

The white cat hesitated for a moment, gripping his spear. He looked at the stranger through a red mist.

"Drop the spear,"demanded the stranger again.

"Back off!" hissed the white cat, "or I'll put YOU down!"

Without waiting he sprang at the stranger, thrusting wildly with the spear. In a fluid movement the stranger dodged the attack. With a swipe of his enormous paw he grabbed the spear from his young enemy. The white cat was helpless as the stranger held him by the scruff of the neck.

Guards rushed to the scene of the fight, calling for help. Soon we were surrounded by a ring of spears with sharp bright tips that glinted like pirates' teeth.

An old white cat with a golden sword came forward.

"What are you doing Romans?" he demanded.

"I'm no Roman," said the stranger. "I'm from the forests of Purrmania.

"Let my son go, if you value your life!" snapped the white cat, his paw on his sword.

I saw the resemblance. Father and son had the same snow white coats and orange eyes. The father glared at the stranger. He was not frightened – he had ten or more guards at his command. He eyed the spear in the stranger's paw.

"By law, I should kill you now for bringing a weapon to the Olympuss gate."

Without thinking, I heard myself saying: "That weapon belongs to your son."

The old white cat turned towards me with a look of disbelief.

"Don't shake your head," I said. "I saw it. Hissing at me won't change the truth of my words. Your son threw the first punch and then went for my friend with that spear. Your guards gave the spear to him."

This disappointing news sucked the pride out of the father. He turned to the young guard, shaking his head sadly. Then he turned and glared at his son.

"Is this true Demawtrius?" he demanded.

A cloud snaked across the sun. The golden spears lost their shine. The son didn't want to look into his father's eyes.

"He challenged me father..." moaned the angry Demawtrius. "I admit that I may have answered his challenge... too quickly."

I could not hold my tongue.

"Too quickly?" I scoffed. You got your first blow in before Maxi had finished talking," I protested. "And then you tried to spear him when he was down on the ground. We came here for sport, not war."

Demawtrius shook his head and glared back at us, his tail flicking.

His father, who was named Periklaws, turned away and spoke to the circle of guards and passers by.

"The Lords of Olympuss are watching us. They expect to see a fair fight," he said.

With a wave of the paw, he ordered the guards to lower their weapons.

"Go in peace, Purrmanian," he said. "You are under the protection of Periklaws."

The hooded stranger acknowledged Periklaws with a nod. Then, turning to the son he added:

"Your father has given you some good advice," he said. "I'd take it if I were you."

There was something very familiar about the stranger's voice.

As Maxi got to his feet, the young white cat was still protesting. But Periklaws was having none of it.

"As for you...," he hissed.

"Sorry father. I was afraid he would have defeated me," insisted Demawtrius.

"You defeated yourself," said his father walking away.

I felt a heavy paw on my shoulder and turned around. The big Purrmanian had removed his hood.

"Wulfren!" cried Maxi in delight. "What in Paws' name are you doing here!"

We had not seen our instructor since the gladiator school.

"Baby sitting you two by the look of it," said Wulfren. I smiled but Wulfren had a straight face.

"I could have taken Demawtrius," protested Maxi. "He caught me by surprise, that's all."

"Have you forgotten your training? You should always be ready for an attack," said Wulfren.

"Don't worry," said Maxi. "I'll show that big white fur ball a few moves when we meet in the games."

Wulfren let out a long sigh.

"His father was right about one thing: compete with honour. Remember you are supposed to be boxing at the Olympuss games – it's not a street fight."

Maxi nodded. Wulfren didn't seem to be

quite as pleased to see us, as we were to see him. But I fancied that I saw a gleam in his eye, despite his gruff greeting.

"I'm here to give you these," he said, passing us a small leather bundle wrapped with a brown string.

Maxi had his open first.

"Silver leaves!" he gasped.

"A present from Father Felinious," he said. "As you've found out, no one gets into the athletes' village without them."

I noticed that Wulfren held a third leather bag in his paw.

"Where's Furia?" he asked.

"Back at the ship with Felinious I think," said Maxi.

Wulfren shook his head.

"Felinious said the three of you had run off together," explained Wulfren.

"She's not with us," said Maxi.

"What's she doing? She'll miss the games," I gasped. "We've got to find her."

Maxi's tail began to flick.

"Can't we get our names down for the games first? And then go and look for Furia?" suggested Maxi.

Wulfren gave him another withering

look.

"I'll take that as a no," muttered Maxi.

"Furia must be found," said Wulfren.

"She could be anywhere," sighed Maxi. He was about to speak again but he gulped his words back down.

I searched the faces of the crowd but there was no sign of Furia.

A long line of carts rumbled down the path towards the gate of Olympuss. Padding alongside them were followers and fans from every nation of the Feline Empire. Although in fact, these games were older than the empire itself. You could breathe in the excitement of the crowd, or at least I think it was excitement – they put a lot of garlic in their fish over here.

By now it was late morning. The sun had won its battle with the clouds and burned them all away. Now it was standing on top of its podium and blazing like a champion. The queue at the gate was getting longer and longer. I turned away from the chattering crowd and looked into the distance. A line of dark blue hills marched across the horizon. And amongst these stony dwarves stood one lonely giant: a high mountain, its shoulders dusted with snow.

"Mount Olympuss!" I said. "That's where we'll find Furia."

Wulfren didn't look convinced. He stood in silence, gazing towards the mountain.

"She found a poem," I explained, in answer to his unspoken question. "The poem talked about 'The white tipped Mount'. Furia must have climbed Mount Olympuss. She's looking for..."

I stopped in mid sentence, like a bird taken cleanly by a hunter's arrow.

"Go on. What is she looking for on Mount Olympuss?" asked Wulfren.

It was a fair question. There was a long awkward silence as the three of us looked at the snow covered mountain.

"Sorry Wulfren, but I'm afraid I can't say," I said. "I swore I'd keep it secret."

I thought Wulfren was going to demand answers. But my old instructor accepted this without any bristling or tail thumping. He let out a sigh.

"Alright," he said. "You two go to the mountain," he ordered. "If you can't find Furia then get back before the sun rises tomorrow. Good fortune!"

And with that he started to stalk off.

"Hang on? Where are you going?" called Maxi.

"Back to the port," replied Wulfren. "If Furia has run off again, she'll need a ship."

No more words were needed, and Wulfren moved off. But after three paces he stopped and added. "Whatever happens, return by sunrise tomorrow... or your dream will be over."

After Wulfren had left, Maxi looked at the queue at the gate. It was getting longer. I knew what he was thinking.

"Come on!" I ordered, "Let's go."

I pulled Maxi away from the queue and onto the path.

The Thin White Path

Two hours passed and we padded onwards up the white stones. If you looked carefully at the top of the mountain, you could see a thin white ring below the snow line. Squinting, I saw that it was a stone wall. My eyes are better than Maxi's and I could make out what looked like a temple carved into the rock. Not surprisingly, we'd found no sign of Furia on our way up the mountain.

Maxi was having second thoughts. He kept looking back down the path, the way we'd come. Far below us what looked like a line of tiny ants were waiting at the gate. You didn't need a Moracle to know what he was thinking.

"We're supposed to be a team," I said.

Maxi nodded.

"Well done for not blabbing to Wulfren about Furia's quest," he added.

It was strange. A part of me had wanted to tell Wulfren about Furia's search for the straybos – the little metal charms that she wore on her collar. They were the thing that had brought us here to Mount Olympuss.

"I did think about telling Wulfren about the quest," I said, puffing a bit as the path got steeper and steeper. "I have the feeling he knows something about it already. Otherwise why did he send us to look for her?"

"Spartan," said Maxi. "Sometimes you really are as thick as a bath house brick! Of course Wulfren wants us to find Furia. She's an escaped slave! She belongs to

Felinious. She's valuable property. That's why he wants to get her back."

"There's more to it than that," I said.

Maxi didn't look convinced.

"When Demawtrius had you at spear point, Wulfren saved your life," I added.

Maxi's tail flicked as he thought about the incident. But then he began to laugh.

"What's so funny?" I asked.

"Perhaps the old wolf thinks we don't stand a chance of winning anything in the games without Furia in our team," he said.

Wild Flowers

As the path wound upwards towards the top of the mountain, the air got colder. The light was crisper too. Insects buzzed on the tiny purple wildflowers that grew along the track. Far below us, those busy ants were still scurrying around and queuing up at the gate. Like the Heroes of Olympuss, we looked down from the mountain and wondered. Instead of pondering about great matters, Maxi and I were wondering if we'd make it back before sunrise, to take part in the games.

I peered upwards. Soon we would be up there on the roof of the world. The air was getting thinner. For a moment I thought I was dreaming as the sound of music drifted towards me.

"Hello kitten, hello kitten!" sang a voice as clear as a mountain stream. Then the music stopped as suddenly as it had started.

"You know what's wrong with your songs?" mused another voice.

"What?" replied the singer.

"They all sound too happy. No one likes happy songs these days, try something sadder."

"Goodbye kitten, goodbye kitten!" sang the clear voice, with exactly the same melody as before.

Maxi, who was ahead of me, was the first to meet the musicians.

"Salve my friends!" he began, and I wondered if the two strangers could speak Catin. Luckily, they could.

"What are you two doing up here?" asked the musician, putting down his lyre.

"We are searching for a female," said

Maxi.

"Aren't we all?" sighed the singer.

"She's about your height, with orange eyes. She answers to the name of Furia."

"She might not answer to any name," I added. "She's not very polite."

The singer shook his head.

"Sorry friend, we've not seen anyone up here. Not even a dormouse for the eagles to feed on. You may as well go back now you've reached journey's end."

He pointed with his paw. I saw that the white stone path ended in a white rock wall. They were big on white in this place.

Maxi sprang up the wall and landed cleanly on the flat rock.

"Where in the name of Peus does he think he's going?" said the musician.

"Don't worry about him. He's a tourist and he likes mountain views," I lied.

The musician strummed a lonely chord on his instrument.

"It's a great view," said the singer, "But the punishment is death if you go near the temple at the top. You do know that don't you?"

"Of course we do," I lied again.

I was dying to ask them about the mysterious forbidden temple at the top of the mountain. But asking questions was going to look suspicious.

The musician called to his friend.

"Time we were off," he said. "We need to get back before they close the gate to the athletes' village. Walk down with us if you'd like some company."

"Thanks, but we're a bit tired," I lied for the third time. "We'll catch you up," I called.

"Suit yourself," said the singer.

The two musicians padded off down the path.

The Temple of Olympuss

As soon as the musicians were out of sight, I followed Maxi up the cliff path towards the forbidden temple.

"Hey Spartan," warned Maxi. "Watch your step, the stones are loose."

On the other side of the rock was a steep drop, a few gnarled trees and then an overhang above the vast boulder field half a mile below. You wouldn't want to fall down there, nine lives or none.

I turned my face up towards where Maxi was climbing. High above him a castle of white clouds opened its gates. I could see Maxi ahead of me, inching his way up the cliff. A fantail of loose stones and gravel rolled down the cliff behind him. My father told me never to look down, and when I looked down, I knew the reason why. Far below I could see tiny orange dots which I realised were camp fires.

Maxi had noticed them too.

"Just our luck!" he moaned. "There they all are, dancing and feasting. And we're stuck up here like a couple of lonely mountain goats."

"Come on," I said, setting off again. "Let's find Furia and get back before sunrise."

We didn't want to admit it, but it was already getting dark. The sun had dropped below the peak of Mount Olympuss. A silver half moon hung in the clear sky.

Ignoring the musician's warning, we made straight for the forbidden temple.

We'd already scaled its outer wall. The ancient temple itself was set high in the rock. We stopped for a rest by an old marble statue. The statue was unrecognisable. Years of wind and weather had rubbed the features off its face.

"Ready Spartan?" asked Maxi.

But I wasn't listening. I'd noticed some paw prints in the soft ground where we stood.

"Hey Spartan!" called Maxi. "Wake up."

When I looked in the direction that Maxi was pointing, I didn't like the look of what I saw. The open plain felt exposed.

"What's the matter? Don't they teach you how to climb mountains in Sparta?" laughed Maxi. "Too busy teaching their kids to steal eh?"

I ignored this comment. My eyes were on Maxi's pack. I looked twice, because I couldn't believe what I was seeing. The pack was glowing with a red light.

"Er... I think you'd better take your pack off," I suggested.

Maxi unslung the leather pack and gasped. It looked like he was carrying a blacksmith's furnace. Red and orange sparks shot from inside.

"What do we do now?" said Maxi,

eyeing the pack suspiciously.

I had no ideas so I kept quiet. But suddenly an ancient voice called from the bag. The beam of Affleana had found its voice again.

"Who's there?" it called.

"It's Maxipuss and the Spartan," answered Maxi.

I sighed. He really wasn't going to stop this stupid Spartan nickname business.

"We found you on the beach – remember?" I added.

Maxi loosened the cover of his pack so that the end of the beam was exposed.

"The finders," muttered the beam. "My memory gets so misty these days."

"I'm actually the finder," said Maxi. "I found you and the Spartan here helped me..."

I gave Maxi a dig in the ribs.

"We're looking for our missing friend Furia," I said.

Maxi's tail flicked. He always liked to take the lead when talking to the beam.

"Where am I?" it whispered.

"Near the top of Mount Olympuss," snapped Maxi, beating me to it.

"On the hill of Krownos!" exclaimed the beam in a worried voice. An arc of red sparks crackled from the bag. The beam burned with a pulsing smokeless fire. I noticed that although it seemed to burn, the grey wood was not consumed by the flame.

"Would you mind not flaming like that?" asked Maxi politely. "Our quest is kind of... secret."

The beam did not answer, but no more sparks came. Its fire had died down. Now it glowed red like a wolf's eyes, caught by a hunter's torch.

"What's wrong with the beam?" I whispered to Maxi. "It doesn't sound too pleased to be here,"

"Finders!" commanded the beam. "You have brought me home..."

"*Finder*, you mean," interrupted Maxi. "I am the one who found you. The Spartan just helped."

Maxi was so annoying! But I held my tongue.

There was an awkward silence. My eyes were drawn to the glowing red light.

"Is this really your home?" asked Maxi.

"I thought you grew up in a forest. You're made of wood."

"Of course I was grown in a forest!" snapped the beam. "But here in the temple on the hill of Krownos, I was given my voice."

"Ah," nodded Maxi. "That makes sense."

He gave me a baffled look. The beam cleared its throat and continued.

"As we climb the hill of Krownos, you'll hear sounds that will tear the courage from your hearts. Myths and monsters will march before your disbelieving eyes. But whatever you see, do not take me out of this bag. Even if your lives depend on it. Do you swear?"

Maxi and I looked at each other in disbelief.

"Swear!" demanded the beam, spitting out a plume of red sparks that lit up the night sky like a temple.

"All right! We swear!" hissed Maxi. "But try to stop sparking like that! There might be guards nearby."

Suddenly, I had an idea.

"Beam," I began, "Can you tell us

who made these tracks in the mud?"
I moved the pack over to the muddy patch
where I'd seen the paw prints before.

"They were made by the friend that you
seek," announced the beam.

"Is she inside the temple?" asked Maxi.

There was a long silence. At last the
beam spoke.

"She is near," said the beam. "Now
wrap me up and tie up the pack. I must try
to sleep."

We did as the beam told us. Maxi
shouldered the pack and we set off in the
direction of the temple.

"This is going to be dangerous," I
whispered.

"Come on Spartan, how hard can it
be?" laughed Maxi. And he sprang off
towards the gate.

"Wait!" I cried. "There's something I
have to tell you."

Maxi hadn't been there to hear the
musicians warn me about the punishment
of 'death' that would fall upon anyone
found near the temple. But it was too late
to stop him. He was already springing
from stone to stone like a mountain goat

on a mission for Mewpiter.

I ran fast to catch up with him. But as I arrived at the stone gate Maxi was already face to face with a guard. The solider wore a uniform unlike anything I'd seen back in Rome. His collar was golden and his helmet was decorated with what looked an owl perching on its crest.

His gold tipped spear was pointed straight at Maxi's throat.

"So to sum up, you are saying that you won't let me in and your orders are to kill strangers on sight?" said Maxi, taking a step backwards. The guard glared at Maxi.

"Who are you?" he demanded. "Who dares to come to Krownus' temple?

While the guard was speaking, Maxi was unshouldering the pack with the beam still inside it.

"Who am I?" boomed Maxi. "I am a Moracle. I can tell the future. And I predict that your near future is going to be... PAINFUL!"

Before the words had left his mouth he'd swung the heavy pack into the face of the guard. It connected with a crack. The big guard dropped like a brick down a well.

"Nice one Maxi!" I sighed, examining the pack to see if the beam was damaged.

"What?" said Maxi in a wounded voice. "I didn't take the beam out of the bag, did I?"

But to my horror, I saw the tell-tale red glow coming from Maxi's pack. Worse still, the guards' bronze helmet was fizzing with a red fire. The sparks were falling in a spider's web around the owl design on the crest of the helmet.

"What's that?" I gasped in horror.

"The owl is the ancient symbol of the city of Cathens," said Maxi, not wanting to miss the chance to show off his knowledge. "This guard must be from Cathens..."

But then Maxi let out a loud scream. The green sparks had worked their magic and now the bronze owl was flapping its metal wings and swooping at us.

"Aaarrrghh!" he screamed. The angry bronze bird pecked Maxi hard on the nose. Maxi let out a cry, snatched up the pack and smashed it down hard on his winged foe with a thud.

"Flap off!" cried Maxi in triumph as he swatted the bird out of the air.

But rather than grounding his enemy, there was another fountain of sparks as the pack connected with the bird. The metal owl seemed to drink in the beam's power. The owl's claws extended, transforming into wicked looking tallons. Before I knew what had happened, the owl had doubled in size before our disbelieving eyes.

"For Peus sake Maxi!" I hissed. "What have you done?"

"It's not my fault. It's the BEAM!" cried Maxi. "It's out of control."

The metal creature tried out its powerful new wings and rose into the air, letting out a warning cry that echoed towards the temple.

"It's because we are on the hill of Krownus," I said. "The magic gets stronger the nearer we get to Olympuss. The beam warned us, but as usual you didn't listen to anything anyone says."

"So what if I like to follow my own advice?" snapped Maxi.

Before I could reply, things went from bad to worse. A second guard rushed towards us. He was armed with a round shield and a long spear.

"Surrender or die!" he hissed.

Neither Maxi or I answered his challenge. We were both staring at the winged lion on the crest of his helmet.

"What in the name of Klaws is that thing on top of his helmet?" I asked.

"A sphinx," said Maxi.

"A sphinx? I thought they were Flegyptian," I snapped.

"They are. But they are also from the Squeak island of Chios. It's one of the largest military islands of the..."

"For Peus' sake! Whatever you do, don't hit him on the head," I pleaded.

The guard with the lion sprang forward and smacked Maxi hard on the face with the shaft of his spear.

"Miaooowch!! That's got to hurt!" I said sympathetically.

Before I could help, the guard had followed up the blow and wrestled Maxi to the ground. The brute had Maxi pinned down and now was forcing the wooden shaft of his spear under Maxi's collar, choking the life out of him. Maxi tried to wriggle free but the guard was relentless.

In a panic, I looked around for something to help. There were no weapons nearby so I sprang onto the guard's back. I clawed and scratched and tried to bite him, but it was no use. It was like taking on an armoured rock. Nothing I tried could free Maxi from the guard's choke hold. My friend's eyes went cloudy and his struggles became weaker. Still the guard pressed the spear shaft down into his neck.

There was nothing for it. With a hiss of rage I grabbed the pack and brought it down on the guard's head with full force.

I knew he'd felt it, because his bronze helmet rang like a temple bell. Not leaving off for a moment I smashed him again. His death grip on Maxi relaxed for a moment.

My friend gasped and choked, clutching at his neck.

"Let go of him!" I cried, swinging the pack and crowning my opponent for a third time. His eyes flickered out like a snuffed candle. Then he fell unconscious on the ground. I was wondering whether to smash him one more time to seal the deal when to my horror, I saw that the pack was glowing with a tell-tell red fire. Sparks arced from the beam and were clustering around the sphinx design on the fallen guard's helmet. Seconds later, a tiny flying lion flapped its bronze wings and let out a quiet roar. The beam had brought the sphinx to life!

I'll say one thing for Maxi. When he gets knocked down, he never stays down for long. By now he was on his feet, bristling with righteous rage and staring daggers at the little bronze lion that was doing its best to roar at him. Maxi snatched the beam out of the pack. I could not believe it. Surely he was not going to smash the sphinx, after what had just happened to the owl?

"For Peus sake don't touch that creature" I warned. "Touch it with the beam and it'll double in size."

"Relax Spartan!" said Maxi, swatting off another attack with his paw "I'm not nearly as stupid as you look."

Beam in paw, Maxi sprang towards a statue. I noticed this statue had a design carved into its base: a cat releasing a dove from a cage. Before I could protest, Maxi pressed the end of the beam into the cage. Soon the red sparks did their work. The bronze cage came into life. It burst from the base of the statue and a silver bird flew twittering up into the sky.

Maxi seized the cage, opened the door and batted the tiny sphinx to the ground with his firm right paw. Quickly he stuffed the fallen sphinx into the cage and slammed the cage door shut.

"There! I've solved the riddle of the sphinx!" he laughed.

He was obviously very pleased with himself for coming up with this clever joke.

The sphinx flapped its wings and clawed

the bars and roared but it could not escape.

"Well done," I said. "But for the love of Paws please put that beam away now!"

Maxi looked at the beam in his paw. High above us there was a squawk and something fell past my nose and landed at the base of the statue. I picked it up. It was a tiny silver feather. Looking up I saw the little silver bird, held by the talons of a triumphant bronze owl.

Maxi padded off. Without waiting a second longer, I followed him up the path. As I dashed towards the next gate, I kept my eye out for more guards. The tower we came to wasn't guarded but a heavy oak gate blocked our way. I looked up to the sky but there was no sign of our friend the bronze owl.

There was a tiny door in the oak gate.

"Ready Spartan?" whispered Maxi, taking hold of the brass handle.

Maxi pulled. The door swung gently open. Creeping through the doorway, I found myself on a narrow path lined with statues. It stretched as far as my eyes could see. Maxi padded towards a statue, taking care not to get too close with the bag containing the beam.

"Are those statues of the heroes of Olympuss?" I asked.

"Looks like it," said Maxi.

Maxi t a closer look.

He had stopped in front of a statue of an enormous dog. Its stone teeth were as long as dinner knives. And it had three sets of them! Its black eyes were colder than the grave.

"Furrburus," gasped Maxi. "The three headed dog that guards the underworld."

I let out a mew of horror as three sets of stone eyes bored into me. Hades' little helper was only a block of black marble. But there was a deadly intent in the statue's cold eyes. Whoever carved this thing must have had nightmares for months.

"Step away from the dog Maxi," I whispered.

Maxi laughed.

"I'm serious Maxi. Whatever happens, don't use the beam. Even if the whole Squeak army comes through the next gate. It's too dangerous. I don't want the beam anywhere near that marble monster."

"Monsters," corrected Maxi. "I don't want to worry you Spartan but there's a whole quarry full of nightmares up here."

Maxi was right. In the bright moonlight I saw that I had a one-eyed giant on my left and a snake-haired horror on my right.

"Promise me that you won't use the beam here," I demanded, my tail flicking in annoyance.

"By the snakes of Mewdusa and my grandmother's golden brush – I swear it. Even if the whole Squeak army comes through the next gate, I swear that I will not use the beam."

I sighed in relief as Maxi stepped into the middle of the path, away from the monstrous statues.

"Happy now?" asked Maxi.

But my happiness was as short lived as an untrained gladiator. It lasted about one minute. Because as we arrived at the next gate, it swung open. And the whole of the Squeak army came charging at us.

Dragon's Teeth

There were lots of them. Too many to count. The moon shone on the crests of their helmets and the points of their spears. Apparently it had taken them a while to get organised. No one had dared to enter the forbidden temple for a hundred summers. But word of our arrival had spread fast – perhaps on the wings of a bronze owl. A cloud of arrows hissed towards us.

Maxi knocked me off my feet and dragged me under a statue. Arrows rattled off the statue's stoney shield.

Maxi poked his head out and pulled it

back in quickly. A spear crashed into the base of the statue.

"Stop!" I cried. "Let's talk about this..."

But my words were answered by a second shower of arrows. The time for talking was obviously over. The time for shooting had started.

Maxi had a grim expression on his face.

"I hate to do this Spartan," he said as he slipped the bag containing the beam off his shoulder.

"No Maxi! It's too dangerous," I hissed. "You'll get us killed."

"Probably," he agreed. "But we'll take some of them with us."

Before I could stop him he sprang up and ran towards the stone figures opposite as fast as a lightning bolt from Mewpiter. In a panic, I ran after him, dodging arrows and spears. Then I saw that Maxi had stopped by a statue. To my relief it wasn't our old friend Furrburus. It was a statue of a brave looking cat holding a bag over his shoulder. My paw went over my mouth. I saw the unmistakable glow of the beam as Maxi took it out of his pack.

The grey statue glowed a sickly green colour as Maxi carefully touched the stone bag.

"It's working," cried Maxi, as the stone bag turned into soft leather. Maxi snatched the bag from the statue's stone claws and held it up in triumph.

"What's inside the bag?" I asked in amazement.

"Watch and learn Spartan," Maxi laughed. "Watch and learn!"

Maxi dipped his paw into the bag and drew out pawfuls of white objects. One of them fell on the ground next to me. It was curved like a new moon.

"What are they?" I asked.

"Teeth," said Maxi. "Do you remember the legend of Cadpuss?"

A spear clattered into the stonework above me.

"This is no time for a history lesson," I hissed.

"What use is a bag full of teeth against spears and swords?" I moaned. I was crestfallen. I hoped that he'd come up with a better plan than this.

"They're not just any old teeth," announced Maxi proudly. "They are dragon's teeth."

"And we're going to throw them?" I asked.

"Wrong again my Spartan friend," laughed Maxi. "We're not going to THROW them, we're going to SOW them."

Many months later, I learned about the legend of Cadpuss, a prince of Purrsia who, it is said, killed a real live fire breathing dragon. As if dragon bashing was not enough for a day's work he also went in for a spot of dentistry. He pulled the dead dragon's teeth out and collected them in a bag. Later, he would scatter them on the ground like seeds and create an army of soldiers called the Spartoi – who did his bidding. According to Maxi, something similar happened when *The Pawgo's* crew ran into trouble during the search for the Golden Fleas. I must admit that I thought that Maxi was as mad as a Minopaw as he merrily dipped his paw into the leather bag and scattered the white teeth on the ground beneath the olive trees. When the bag was empty, Maxi threw it away and dived for cover.

"What do we do now?" I called.

"We wait," he answered.

I let out a sigh, not daring to stick my head around the base of the statue. The last time I peeped out I was greeted by a hail of arrows. This is the end, I thought. It really won't be long now. Had Furia met a similar fate for daring to break into the forbidden temple? Our dreams of Olympuss were over. I was just about to shout a final curse at Maxi, when the arrows and spears stopped flying. Shouts of panic and fear came from our enemy. Through the confusion, I heard Maxi's voice.

"Spartoi!" boomed Maxi.

"For Peus sake will you stop calling me Spartan?" I hissed. "You never let up with the nicknames, even when the hour of our death is upon us."

"I wasn't talking to you," called Maxi. "I was talking to my Spartoi."

Ever so slowly, I peaked out from behind the base of the statue. In the

54

middle of the path stood a row of thin white figures carrying round shields and long spears.

Not for the first time that day, I looked on in amazement.

"The Spartoi are warriors," called Maxi in delight. "And they're fighting for me!"

"Er, Maxi... there's one problem with your army..."

There was no time to finish the sentence. A patch of ground in front of me rippled, as if someone had thrown a stone into a pool. Slowly, the bronze blade of an ancient sword poked up from the red earth. The sword was being gripped by a boney paw. I gasped as the skeleton of the warrior rose from the earth and stared to shake the dirt from its bones. Pausing only to dig up its helmet and place it upon its skull, it rattled over to join the ranks of its companions.

"Problem? What problem?" called Maxi.

"Your warriors appear to be dead," I hissed.

"That's not a problem," laughed Maxi. "They can't be killed because they're dead already. Aren't you lads?"

I grudgingly had to admit that he had a point. The temple guards had clearly boned up on their myths and legends. As soon as the first warriors were out of the ground they had run like rabbits. Maxi's skeleton army had scared them off. Now the place was deserted. There was just me, Maxi and his skeleton crew.

Something whizzed past my nose like a shooting star. Rather unsportingly, the guards had started to fire flaming arrows at us (from a safe distance). One of Maxi's new recruits was hit in the eye socket. His skull started to blaze like a gatekeeper's torch. This didn't bother the boney warrior. He kept walking towards the spot where the arrow had come from, his gladius still in his burning paw.

"What now?" I asked, getting up from my hiding place to joining Maxi by the Furrburus statue.

Maxi had a broad smile on his face.

"I think that thanks are in order," he said.

"Thank Mewpiter we're alive," I said.

"You should be thanking me Spartan," he laughed. "We're still breathing. And we never had to wake this three headed puppy after all."

He pointed his sword at the statue of Furrburus – the three headed hound of Hades.

"Thank you Maxi," I said sarcastically.

"You couldn't win a fight with a three legged dog – let alone a three-headed one!" he added.

There was no time to think up a witty reply. While we had been talking, the temple guards had stopped firing. Everything had gone quiet. In horror, I realised that Maxi's skeleton army had stopped fighting the guards. They'd formed up in neat ranks, facing us. At the head of the ranks of Spartoi warriors, stood a pale figure. He was taller than all the rest and armed with a long spear with a rusty tip. In the darkness I saw that green fires burned in the sockets where the eyes of this skeleton king had once been. He marched towards us, clutching the spear in his boney paw.

I wondered if he was an illusion – a thing of magic, or whether this creature had ever chased a mouse or tasted fresh fish or basked in the sunlight. But these thoughts vanished like morning mist when he pointed the spear at Maxi.

"Maxi..." I whispered. "We ought to be going."

"Nonsense!" said Maxi. "They are MY warriors and they'll obey me."

"Spartoi!" boomed Maxi. "Hear the words of your commander: Maxipuss the Magnificent..."

In one fluid movement the warriors turned towards Maxi.

"I think you've got their attention..." I

hissed.

Then the skeleton warriors raised their swords and spears and started to advance slowly towards us.

"I command you to HALT!!!" cried Maxi in his best impression of Wulfren, our instructor back at the gladiator school.

But Maxi's parade ground performance wasn't working on these recruits. The first rank of the skeleton army broke out and came running towards us swinging their swords and brandishing their spears.

"Er, Maxi..." I began. "Your new recruits don't like following orders. What do we do now?"

Maxi wore a wounded look on his face.

Snatching up a spear, I ran and hurled it at the army of skeletons. To my surprise, it was the perfect throw. By some twist of fortune my spear arrowed through the air, straight towards the head of the skeleton king. There was a smash of steel on bone as the spear tore into its skull. The other skeletons stopped dead in their tracks. Maxi turned to me with a look of joy and jealousy on his face.

"Good throw Spartan!" he cried. "You knocked old boney's block off!"

For a moment I felt like a hero: a champion of Olympuss. But my dreams of winning the javelin competition were over in a flash.

With a creak and a rattle, the skeleton king got back up and went searching for his missing skull. I watched in horror as he found it and screwed it back onto his neck with a crunch of bone on bone. He glared at me, grinding his teeth and spitting a loose one out.

"For Peus sake!" I moaned. "What have I done?"

"Old Boney doesn't look too pleased with you Spartan," said Maxi in a worried voice. "You'd better flee. I'll hold them off here."

"Hold them off?" I hissed. "How in Paws' name are you going to do that?"

My heart sank. The skeleton king was reaching for his spear. Time froze as I watched my enemy draw back its arm. The spear came flying straight towards me at eye level. I wanted to move but my paws felt like they were made of solid stone. If Maxi hadn't pulled me to the ground, the spear would have skewered me like a rat kebab.

There was a glow of disappointment in the green eye sockets of my dead opponent when he saw that he'd missed.

"One more thing," said Maxi. "If he asks for his spear back – don't give it to him."

The skeleton king opened his jaws and began to chatter what was left of its teeth. I think it was trying to curse me, but it had no tongue to curse with. So it strode towards me, sword held high in its dead paw.

"Don't stand there like a dog that's forgotten where it buried its bone," Maxi yelled. "Run Spartan!"

His words broke the spell and I sprang up, ready to run for my life. I was about to flee when something stopped me. I turned towards Maxi. He was reaching into the pack containing the magic beam.

"Talking of bones..." he laughed. "Maybe it is time to let the dog out?"

A cold cloud of dread passed over

me as I looked up at the cursed three-headed statue and then towards the army of advancing skeletons. Dogs and bones! I knew exactly what Maxi had in mind. This was no time to be caught cat napping.

"Wait here," cried Maxi advancing towards the statue of Furburrus.

Every ticking second seemed to last for hours. I noticed that my mouth was open, so I closed it. In gladiator school they taught me that heroes don't dribble.

The thin clouds lifted and a column of silver moonlight lit the statue opposite my hiding place. This latest statue was of a cloaked figure with a bent back. In its right paw, it carried a sickle: the sort of curved tool with a long handle that a gardener uses for cutting grass. The way I am describing it, the ancient statue sounds rather creepy. In the moonlight it actually looked rather beautiful. Then the clouds covered the moon again and darkness returned.

Looking up into the night, I saw a dark shape approaching. I held my breath. But it was just a crow. It flew up and perched

KROWNVS

on the statue's shoulder. But it had to leave its new perch in a hurry. A spark of green lightning pierced the night. This was followed by a fountain of hot sparks shooting out of the beam in Maxi's shaking paw.

I dived for cover as a howling noise shook the calm night. My worst fears had come true. Furrburus had woken up.

So far, using the beam had not been
a good idea. I won't say that we hadn't
been warned. First, Father Felinous had
told us about the danger. Then we'd seen
it with our own eyes at the Tower of the
Winds. Finally, the beam itself had begged
us to be careful. We'd sworn not to
remove it, even if our lives were in danger.

Sometimes it is hard to admit when
you've made a mistake but if I could turn
back time on the hill of Krownus then
I surely would. I knew that what Maxi
had done was madness of the very worst
order. Trying to cure chaos with more
chaos. However, I do not blame Maxi for
a second. The temple guards would have
killed us, if it wasn't for his quick thinking. He had sown the dragon's teeth and
created an army that had driven away
the temple guards. But violence breeds
violence. Now he needed a bigger, badder
monster than the skeleton army. So he'd
turned to Hades' little helper: Furrburus.
According to the legends, this three-
headed hound guards the gates of the

underworld. Whether the dog's job was to keep the tourists out, or keep the residents in, I have no idea. As I'd crept past the statue of the three-mouthed monster it had set my tail flicking. It wasn't the two extra heads, or the teeth like butcher's blades; it was the cold glare of the creature's eyes. It was cast out of pure evil. The evil paw that made it had added a pinch of cold hate and a dash of hot spite to its metal. My heart was clanging like a miner's hammer as I ran in terror from its growls.

Maxi had the good sense not to stand between a dog and its bone (or between a three headed hound and a skeleton army). The instant that the beam's sparks touched Furburrus statue, he had run for cover like Purrcury – the flying messenger – on a 24 hour delivery. Peeping out from behind his statue, he narrowly avoided getting caught by the glare of one of the creature's three heads. For Furrburus was a watch dog, and could keep a look out in three directions at once. At the moment his three monstrous heads weren't doing much watching. They were busy chomping up skeleton warriors like a senator at an all-you-can eat fish buffet.

My old aunt Carapuss used to love eating crabs. She would crack the poor creatures to pieces with a silver hammer and suck out the white meat. The terrible crunching noise I heard now was like aunty Cara on a crab feast, but worse. Unlike the crabs, who had been boiled to death before the cracking started, the Spartoi didn't like the idea of being cracked to pieces. Soon they were mounting a counter attack on our three-headed friend. Not that it did them much good. Furrburus snatched up warrior after skeleton warrior with its three mouths. Its great heads shook from side to side as it bit down hard. I looked on in awe as one by one, the army of skeletons were shaken to pieces.

A voice at my side made me jump.

"Maxi!" I gasped. "Thank Peus you're safe!"

My friend had picked his moment and followed me away from the bone cracking scene.

But Maxi looked worried.

"What's wrong?" I asked.

"Nothing, except the obvious...." he replied, waving a paw in the direction of Furrburus.

I studied his express for a moment before finally asking.

"Are you hurt?"

Maxi shook his head.

"Turn around, let's have a look at you," I ordered.

"It's nothing," he protested.

There was a patch of fur missing from his flank and he was bleeding.

"It's not too bad," I said. "You've taken worse wounds in the arena."

Maxi looked like he'd seen a ghost.

"It's not that..." he began.

Unlike me, my friend was an expert on all things Squeak. Maxi knew every myth and legend of these islands. I wondered what was troubling him.

"Out with it!" I ordered. "There's something bothering you I can tell, so you may as well let me in on it."

Maxi was as silent as the grave.

"Let me guess," I began cheerily. "The weapons of the Spartoi are poisoned?"

"Nope," said Maxi.

"Or cursed?" I guessed.

"Wrong again Spartan," sighed Maxi. "Although I may as well have been cursed."

"Come on!" I laughed, slapping him on the back. "It can't be as bad as that..."

"It's Furrburus," said Maxi. "As I was sneaking away, one of his three heads spotted me. I rolled for cover when he bit me."

"And you're alive?" I gasped. "How did you escape?"

Maxi shrugged his shoulders.

"I think I must have slipped between his teeth."

"You have the luck of Paws himself!" I cried. "You were bitten by Furrburus and yet you're here to tell the tale."

Maxi looked over his shoulder. After a long silence he reluctantly began to speak.

"They say that if Furrburus tastes your blood, then there's no stopping him."

I'd never heard Maxi sound this serious before. As I bandaged up his wound, he winced and then went on speaking in an quiet voice.

"The legend says that if Hades' hound has your scent he'll track you to the ends of the earth..."

He sat still while I pulled the bandage tight. This was bad. It could hardly get any worse.

"...And drag you down to the Underworld."

Was the legend true? Or was it just a tale to frighten the kittens? It wasn't wise to wait around and find out. Somewhere in the distance we heard an unmistakable growl.

"Come on," he said. "We're getting out of here right now."

"Wait!" I hissed, grabbing his collar. "You're going the wrong way."

"No," he insisted. "YOU are going the wrong way Spartan. The games are down there."

Maxi pointed to the path leading back down the mountain. "That... hell hound is back up there somewhere," he said softly. "And it has my scent," he hissed. I had never seen Maxi look this frightened before. He was standing very still, as if he was trying to blend into the scenery, which would have been hard seeing as his fur was standing on end like the bristles on a brand new toothbrush.

"But what about Furia?" I insisted. "If we leave Mount Olympuss without finding her then we'll have risked our lives for nothing. We swore to help her with the quest."

Maxi looked shocked. In all the chaos he had completely forgotten about finding Furia. He felt a pang of shame.

"You're right Spartan," he said in a grim voice. "But... we can't just march back up into the jaws of Furrburus. It's a death mission."

"Give me the pack," I said. "I've just thought of something."

I set off up the path with a heavy heart and the pack with the magic beam in my paw.

To keep one promise, I'd have to break another. To honour my promise to help Furia on her quest, I'd have to break my promise not to use the beam.

A Three-Headed Friend

"That one in the middle?" I whispered, examining the row of statues.

Maxi's mouth moved when he answered. But he was speaking so quietly that I couldn't make out what he was saying. I looked in the direction of his outstretched paw and gasped. Her silhouette was unmistakable.

"I'll do it," hissed Maxi.

"No,' I replied. "It's my turn. It's your job to lure Furrburus down here."

Furrburus probably wouldn't need very much luring, to tell the truth. He'd already got the scent of Maxi, and if the legend was true, he'd be drawn to Maxi like an evil three-headed caterpillar to a cabbage patch.

It sounded simple enough. The timing was the hard part. Without another word Maxi sprang out of our hiding place and shot off up the hill in the direction of the howling. I dashed over to the statue of Mewdusa and got into position.

A tell-tale red glow came from the inside of the Maxi's pack. I undid the straps and slowly took out the magic beam. The beam was cold to the touch, but sparks poured out of it like water from a fountain. I noticed that as the first spark hit the marble, it turned green.

I took a step back. I didn't want this to happen too fast. If I woke the sleeping statue too early, I'd be dead before Maxi arrived with Hades' hound on his tail.

"I'm sorry beam," I whispered. "There's just one more monster to wake and then we'll quit."

Then a horrible howl shook the night. Maxi was screaming: "I'm on my way Spartan! Now!"

The beam trembled in my shaking paw. Around the corner came Maxi running for his life. Not far behind him crashed an enormous dog with three sets of teeth like yellow daggers. It snarled and snapped as it bounded out of my nightmares. It crashed down the path on Maxi's tail.

"For Peus sake Spartan!" cried Maxi. "Do it now!"

I gazed up at the statue. Its dark shape loomed over me.

sparks from the beam soaked the base of the statue in a weird light. I noticed that as the sparks hit the marble statue, they changed colour from red to green.

I could feel my fur bristling. This was madness. Carved into the rock at the base of the statue was a single word. a word that would freeze the blood of heroes. The word was: *Mewdusa*.

The changes worked their way from her tail to her head.

First came a creaking noise. Then I heard the grinding of metal on stone. The sparks did their work: the statue of Mewdusa was turning to flesh and fur and claws. Remembering Maxi's warning, I looked away just in time before Mewdusa's green eyes snapped open.

Then the hissing started. A stone snake uncoiled itself, followed by another and another. Soon the top of her head was a nest of snakes, hissing and writhing as if they'd been poked with a sharp stick.

In Mewdusa's green claw was a
long spear. Doubtless, those dreadful
green eyes were glaring with hatred.
But she wasn't glaring at me. For just
as Mewdusa leapt from the base of her
statue, around the corner came Maxi
and snapping at his heels was our three
headed friend Furrburus.

Mewdusa's snakes hissed and spat
poison at the dog's nearest head.
Furrburus skidded to halt. His first head
let out a terrible growl. His second head
was snapping at Maxi. His third head
turned and snarled at the figure with
the spear. But it was too late. Mewdusa
held him by his eyes. I could see each
head fighting her deadly gaze. But it
was no good, try as he might, Furrburus
could not look away. One by one, the
three heads of Furrburus turned to face
Mewdusa. There he stood, staring like
a row of kittens at a fish shop window
– unable to look away. The snakes in
Mewdusa's hair began to coil, they
fell silent and the hissing stopped. Five

seconds later, the growling had stopped too. A new statue stood in the middle of the path. Mewdusa's stare had turned the dog to stone. It was not particularly nice looking stone either – it looked like badly mixed concrete.

Somewhere inside I felt slightly sorry for Hades' hound. Although he had been evil, there was a certain dark glamour about the big three-headed brute.

One of those old wise cats that my father likes once said that every creature, great or small, has the right to live. I'm not sure if this works with evil creatures (like three-headed hounds of Hades). Furrburus was originally a statue, not a living thing. He'd been brought to life by Maxi to destroy the terrible army of Spartoi skeletons. Now Furrburus was a statue again. Maxi had created him and now he would destroy him. This gave me a sinking feeling so I decided to stop thinking about it. As my father says, it's a good idea not to think too much because if thoughts stay in your head too long they come out rotten.

I was torn away from these thoughts by a horrible hissing noise. It is said that readers should not judge a book by its cover. But this book's cover was so horrid, gross, foul and loathsome that any reader would run in panic and give up reading for a nicer hobby, like rat-catching in Rome's main drain on the hottest day of the year. As she drew closer, I saw that Mewdusa's head was too big for her body. The tangle of hissing snakes wasn't helping her look. When she opened her mouth to snarl at the stars, I noticed that her tongue was forked like a snake's. She had clawed feet and a set of teeth that any shark would be proud of. It's safe to say that Mewdusa wasn't going to win the Miss Olympuss beauty contest – snakes or no snakes.

In horror, I realised that now she had finished with Furrburus she was on the hunt for her next victim. Her snakes coiled and twisted, their forked tongues tasting the air for the scent of strangers.

As I watched in terror, my attention

was taken by a sound coming from the opposite side of the pathway. I turned an ear towards the noise. Silently I turned my head to face it. Pressed against the base of a statue was the unmistakeable figure of my friend Maxi. He was completely still. For a horrible moment I thought that our hissy-haired friend had already got him. So I was relieved to see his whiskers twitch. On his face he wore a look of blind terror. Mewdusa was moving menacingly down the path towards him, probing every hiding place with her spear.

In a panic, I struggled to think. I still had the bag with the beam in my paw. My first thought was to use the beam to wake another statue and create a diversion. But as soon as I removed the beam from the pack, its red light would reveal my hiding place.

I crouched in the curved trunk of a twisted tree. At the moment, I was concentrating hard on hiding from Mewdusa. She was the end result, the sum of all of this magical meddling.

The beam's magic had done what we'd wanted. But sometimes it is an unexpected blessing when your deepest wishes are NOT granted.

Maxi had created Mewdusa. She was about to destroy him – and me too. The time for thinking was over. It was time to act. My heart hammered as I untied the bag and took out the magic beam. The grey wood was warm to the touch and it began to glow. Mewdusa was only a few steps away from the spot where Maxi was hiding.

Mewdusa was no fool. She could sense that someone was near. Her snakes hissed and stuck out their tongues, tasting the air and guiding her.

Step followed step. She was two paces away from Maxi. I took a deep breath. Then I stepped out of my hiding place, holding the beam high in the air. Red sparks crackled down the beam and began to fly from its tip.

Mewdusa stopped in her tracks and spun around. But I was ready for her.

I admit that I looked like a fool,

standing there in the middle of the path with a bag over my head. But wearing the beam bag was the only thing I could think of to avoid Mewdusa's deadly gaze. In the legend, Purrseus had used a blindfold, but he'd come prepared.

"Over here!" I cried. "Come and get it."

I heard a loud hiss and not for the first time that night I heard Maxi calling:"Run Spartan!"

Still clutching the beam in my paw, I rolled to the left. Mewdusa's spear jabbed the air where I'd just been standing. Springing up, I held the beam high.

"Is this what you want?" I cried.

I could feel the fat sparks whizzing out of the beam as the hissing of the snakes grew louder.

"Don't give her the beam,"cried Maxi. "Throw it to me!"

I stood with my eyes tight shut, even though I still had the bag over my face. Cautiously, I lifted the bottom of the bag to risk a peak. Looking out, I saw that I was in the centre of a crossroads with side paths on either side.

"To me!" Maxi cried again, beckoning to me to throw him the beam.

I pulled back my arm for a mighty throw. But something stayed my paw. Instead, I turned and sent the beam spinning though the air down one of the side paths.

"Spartan!" moaned Maxi. "What in Paws name are you doing!"

"I'll explain later," I cried. "What's Mewdusa up to? I can't see with this thing on my head."

"She's gone after the beam," hissed Maxi. "But..."

"Well come on then!" I cried. "What are you waiting for?"

But... the beam!" he cried. "We can't just leave it!"

However, at least he'd followed my advice and ran over to join me.

Time To Throw

Despite Maxi's hissing and tail flicking, he followed me up the path.

With Mewdusa lured by the light of the magic beam, Maxi and I took off like a couple of chariot horses on race day. Maxi was still protesting when we reached the temple. He loved that magic beam. It was as if I'd just thrown his grandmother to Mewdusa.

"Using the beam got us into trouble," I said. "Besides – we came here to find Furia. And I have a feeling that this is where we'll find her."

Inside the temple, the lamps were burning down low. We padded softly up the white marble steps and peered through the dancing shadows. The sweet smell of perfume hung in the air.

"Furia!" I called. My voice echoed around the huge space. There was no answer.

'I don't want to worry you Spartan," hissed Maxi. "But I think we've got company."

I span around to see a familiar shape, lit up with a green glow. It was walking slowly up the path in our direction.

"Mewdusa!" I moaned.

"She's following us," I sighed.

"Hunting us is more like it. And now she's got the beam," said Maxi.

He didn't need to rub it in. My heart sank. What had I been thinking?

"Hide!" I cried. "Quickly."

Maxi ran to the lamps and snuffed them out. We took off towards the back of the temple, running like two rats in a pipe. In a panic, I searched for hiding places. The best bet was a line of tall columns heading down each side of the temple. I dived behind a column, but crashed into Maxi who'd obviously had the same idea.

"Not here!" hissed Maxi. "Hide over there! We stand a far better chance if we split up."

He was probably right as usual, but I didn't see why I should be the one who had to move. I let out a yowl as I prepared to move. Then I felt a paw on my shoulder.

"Remember Spartan," whispered Maxi. "Whatever you do, don't look into Mewdusa's eyes. Or they'll be chipping you into your coffin with a chisel."

Nodding, I made a dash for the opposite side of the temple.

But as soon as I stepped out from behind the column, I saw my mistake. Mewdusa was already inside. She stood before me, with a spear in one claw and the beam in the other. Holding the beam like a torch, she edged forward. Her snakes coiled and writhed in the red glow of the beam's light. Muttering curses, I pulled my eyes away from her and backed away. But it was too late. She'd spotted me! The snakes on her hair let out a terrible hiss and began to spit poison in my direction. I felt a dark liquid land on my face. It burned when I wiped my eyes.

As I staggered backwards, I knew that I was caught. Then I noticed something strange. The soft red light of the beam was replaced by a bright yellow light. Peeping to my left I saw that someone had lit the line of lamps. The place blazed with pools of bright light. "Maxi???" I cried. "Is that you?"

At that moment a flash of silver shot past me, there was a dreadful hissing noise, and then... silence.

When I finally got the courage to open my eyes, I saw a figure before me, holding an enormous shield made of highly polished metal.

"Stars of Andrasta!" cried the figure with the shield.

"Furia!!" I gasped. "Thank Paws we've found you."

Furia's shield was so shiny that I could see my face in it. I noticed that my lower jaw had dropped in surprise, so I pulled it up again and tried to stop gawping.

On the other side of Furia, stood the cold grey figure of Mewdusa. She'd been turned into stone by her own evil spell. In her claw, she still held the magic beam. Maxi ran towards her in a panic.

"The beam!" he moaned. "It's been turned to stone!"

"But how...?" I demanded.

"Furia used her shield as a mirror," said Maxi. "As soon as Mewdusa saw her own reflection in the mirrored shield, she got turned to stone. That's how Purrseus killed her in the legend."

Furia nodded.

"Our beam was turned to stone with her," said Maxi sadly.

I put a comforting arm around his shoulder.

"I think the beam knew that something like this was going to happen," I said. "It tried to warn us."

Maxi nodded.

"What are you two fools doing here?" asked Furia.

"Looking for you," I answered. "We said we'd help you with your quest, remember?"

Furia's tale began to flick.

"Were you helping, when you ran off and left me on the ship with Father Felinious?" demanded Furia.

"Sorry about that," I said. "We got kind of carried away about the games."

"Talking of the games," said Maxi. "Let's get moving right now. If Fortune is with us, we can still make it to the village by sunrise and enter the competition."

Furia's tail flicked but said nothing.

"Er... after we've helped Furia with her quest, you mean," I said hastily.

Maxi nodded.

"Of course," said Maxi. "How are you doing with that?" he asked.

"Have you found the last straybo yet?"

I looked at the little metal charms around Furia's collar. I saw that there were still only three. Furia had come to Mount Olympuss to find the fourth straybo.

"It's not here," she said sadly.

"We'll help you to search this temple," I suggested.

"I've searched this place already," she explained.

"How did the rhyme go?" I asked, trying to remember the words of the clue that had brought us on the search. Furia repeated the verses of the poem:

The answer is two times two...
Tick tock tick
climb the white tip mount
Time runs out
Olympuss!

The three of us stood silently for a long while.

"Right!" I said. "We said that the

'white tip mount' is Mount Olympuss. It's a snow capped mountain. The next line of the verse says *Time runs out...* What could that mean?"

Furia didn't reply. Maxi wasn't even listening. He was still staring at his beloved magic beam, high in the stoney claw of Mewdusa.

"Maxi!!" I hissed.

"What?" he muttered, turning to face me.

"Time runs out," I said. "You know all the myths and legends. Was there a legend about Time?"

"Krownus," said Maxi instantly. "He's in charge of time. There must be a statue of Krownus around here somewhere."

"What does Krownus look like?" I asked.

"You can't miss him," explained Maxi. "He's as old as a mountain and he carries a sickle."

I gave Maxi a puzzled look.

"A sickle. You know. A curved blade. The sort of tool that the gardening slaves use to cut flowers."

"Slaves?" I said in surprise. "You have slaves to do your gardens?"

Maxi looked back at me, equally surprised.

"Of course," he said. "We Romans love our gardens."

Furia looked at Maxi, in the way that a snake stares at a baby bird. I thought she was going to hit him with her shiny shield. But instead she just sighed.

"There's no statue of Krownus in here," she said. "I've looked everywhere."

Then an idea popped into my head.

"It's not here!" I said excitedly. "It's a little way back down the path. But there's definitely a statue carrying a sickle back there."

"Are you sure?" asked Furia.

"In Paws' name I swear it is true," I replied. "I was hiding behind it earlier."

Furia gave me a questioning look.

"Lead the way Spartan," ordered Maxi.

The Place Where Time Runs Out

A few minutes later I'd led them to the statue. It should have looked creepy, but there was something unusual about Krownus. It was cast in bronze. A hood covered its eyes. The moonlight danced on the tip of the gardener's sickle. Cast in bronze, Krownus had a fluid quality. He had been caught in mid stride. For an ancient cat, Krownus was light on his paws.

"Why's he running?" I asked.

"Time's always running," said Maxi.

"Time runs out!" exclaimed Furia.

"You're telling me," hissed Maxi, looking down the hill in the direction of the games. Furia gave him a hard stare.

"Krowus stands for Time. His statue is running. This must be the right place. The clue said that 'Time runs out'."

"Search everywhere," I cried. "The missing straybo is here somewhere."

It didn't take long to spot. At the base of the statue was a small hole. It was invisible to passers by but easy to see if you knew what you were looking for. Without delay I edged my paw into the crack and pulled out the final straybo.

"Got it!" I cried in triumph. I held the final straybo in the air as I danced a little dance of victory.

I noticed that the other two were giving me funny looks. So I stopped celebrating and gave the straybo to Furia.

"Great," said Maxi grumpily. I could tell he was secretly annoyed not to have found the last straybo. "Let's move!"

Maxi jumped up and took off down the path.

"Wait!" I cried. "Where are we going?"

There was no clue with the final straybo. We had all four charms but what were we supposed to do with them?

Furia looked at the statue in silence. Tick chased tock. Time was running out. I looked up at the sky. The inky black of midnight had worn thin. Soon the dawn would come knocking. As soon as the sun rose, the Olympuss games would begin, with or without us.

Maxi sighed and his tail began to flick.

"What is it?" I asked.

He looked at me accusingly. "If we still had our beam, we could wake up old Krownus and ask him what to do."

"If wishes were fishes, I'd get my fishing rod out," I sighed.

Maxi's beloved beam was no use to us now it had been turned to stone.

Then I heard it. The unmistakable sound of paws padding towards us up the stone path. I have excellent hearing. Putting my paw over my mouth I warned the other two to be silent. Maxi and Furia stepped back into the shadows. Maxi had his gladius ready to strike. The sound of the steps got louder and louder. Maxi raised his sword, ready to take the stranger as they came around the base of the statue.

"Halt!" he cried. "Take one more step and it will be your last."

"It's nice to see you too, Maxipuss," said a familiar voice.

"Father Felinious!" I cried. "What in the name of Peus are you doing up here?"

"Looking for all of you," sighed Felinious, nodding at Furia. She didn't seem too pleased to see him.

"I see you found Furia for me," he said. "Better late than never, as they say. But where is the beam?"

Maxi looked at me accusingly.

"The beam..." I began. But my words faded into nothing.

"The beam," demanded Felinious. "You know, the magic one that you took without asking."

"It's gone," said Maxi. "Turned to stone."

Maxi carefully explained everything that had happened up to this point. But he missed out the bit where I knocked the head off the skeleton king of the Spartoi with an epic spear throw. When he got to the bit where I threw the beam away to distract Mewdusa, I turned away in shame.

At last Maxi finished telling the story. Felinious was silent for what seemed like an age. I thought he was going to call me a ginger half-wit for throwing away the beam. But instead, I saw a smile on his face. With a dramatic flourish, he swung the pack off his back. At first I couldn't believe it, but there it was before my eyes. The tell-tale red glow coming from inside Felinious' pack gave it away.

"The beam!!!?" I gasped. "But... how can it be? Mewdusa was holding it when she was turned to stone."

"Magic can't work against itself," said Felinious. "The beam's magic created the statue of Mewdusa. It could never be used to turn itself to stone."

We all stared at the old cat in amazement.

"How did you become so wise?" I asked.

"Old straw burns the brightest," laughed Felinious.

"Where did you find it?" purred

Maxi, with the old smile back on his face.

"I found it exactly where you left it," laughed Felinious. "When I came looking for you I went straight to the temple. When I saw a brand new statue of Mewdusa in the middle of the aisle, I guessed what had happened."

Furia, who had been silent through all of this talking, spoke in a serious voice.

"There was no clue with the last straybo," she hissed. "So what now?"

Felinious took a deep breath and looked at Furia.

"I am your final clue my dear," he said. "Follow me and all will be revealed."

"Where are we going?" asked Maxi.

"We're off to find a box," said Felinious.

Maxi and I looked at each other, trying to work out what was going on inside the old cat's mind.

"Where is this box?" Furia asked.

"Periklaws has it," said Felinious.

The Race

Our first race of the Olympuss games was a race against time. It had been decided that Maxi and I would get back to the village as fast as we could. The others would follow as quickly as they could. Maxi was delighted that old Felinious wasn't going to slow us down. He took off like a stone from a sling-shot. I did my best to keep up with him as we blew past the watchtower like the East wind.

As I ran, I could see the sky above us get lighter. Slowly but surely, the night sky was turning the colour of dirty steel. After an hour of running we reached the top of the cliff. I needed to rest. The climb back down the cliff wasn't easy. Maxi looked down the mountain and let out a sigh. Dawn was now faint glow on the horizon, but we were still only half way down the mountain.

I knew it was useless. We'd missed our chance. But I didn't have the heart to tell Maxi.

"Move Spartan!" moaned Maxi, in frustration. He jumped up, ready to run his heart out. Then he stopped.

"What's the matter?" I asked.

"Do you hear that Spartan?" moaned Maxi.

"Did I hear what?" I asked.

"Bird song," sighed Maxi. "It's the dawn chorus. We are too late Spartan. We've missed the Olympuss games."

A Meeting with Periklaws

Maxi's dream of the games was over, but he didn't mew like a spoilt kitten. We all have to fail sometimes – even born winners like Maxi. We knew that there was no hope. The rules said that the gate would be locked 'at the crack of dawn.' Well, dawn had cracked. We had run out of time.

We waited for Furia and Felinious in silence. The gate was guarded by grim faced guards armed with spears and swords. Security was tight at the games.

At last Felinious and Furia arrived. I was impressed that the old cat had managed to make it down so quickly. I was so tired that I found myself dozing off. When I woke up, Furia was whispering something in Maxi's ear. Was she telling him that she was sorry that we'd missed the games?

Felinious padded up to the most important looking guard, a tabby with a thin face and a turned up nose. The tabby tut-tutted when he saw us coming. He was already shaking his head at Felinious as he drew near.

"Take us to Periklaws," demanded Felinious.

The guard's tone was equally high and mighty.

"Periklaws sees no one," he hissed, pointing at gate.

"He'll see me," said Felinious. "Give him this."

Felinious took one of the straybos from Furia's collar and passed it to the guard.

"What is it?" asked the guard, examining the straybo carefully. "If it's a bribe then you'll have to do better than a bit of old bronze," he said. "I like to go for gold."

The other guards laughed but Felinious shook his head.

"If I were you, I'd take that 'bit of old bronze' to commander Periklaws immediately.

Something in Felinious' stone-cold voice made the guards listen.

"Wait here," he ordered.

"Tell Periklaws that there are three more where that one came from," added Felinious.

Ten minutes later the four of us were sitting in Periklaws' tent. The tent was pitched on an area of flat ground high above the arena. Felinious wore a serious expression on his face. Furia's tail flicked nervously against the ground. Far below, the games had started. The tree climbing event was already underway. The crowd were cheering the climbers on. Maxi was looking down longingly at the arena, far below. He was wishing it was him in the arena. Felinious put a friendly paw on his shoulder.

"Courage Maxipuss," he said. "There'll be other games for you."

Before Maxi could reply, a blue curtain at the back of the tent swished open and an old white cat entered with a couple of guards at his tail.

"Periklaws," said Felinious with a curt nod. "How long has it been?"

Behind the white cat came two guards. One of them was carrying a wooden box.

Periklaws held the straybo in his paw. The golden charm gleamed in the morning sun. I noticed that the edge of the straybo was not smooth, but it had a series of small grooves in it, like a cog or a wheel.

"We have searched for this for many years. I had given up hope..." began Periklaws. "Where... did you find it?"

Just as he said these words, his eyes

went to the other straybos on Furia's collar.

"Three more?" gasped Periklaws. "How did you come by them?"

There was a dash of suspicion in the white cat's voice. He sounded amazed and annoyed at the same time, if that is possible. Furia looked at him, not sure if she should answer.

"They were made by Furia's grandmother," explained Felinious.

Furia glared at Felinious.

"Her grandmother?" gasped Periklaws. The guards started to laugh but he silenced them with a wave of his white paw. "That cannot be. Those objects were made long ago, back in the ancient days."

Furia's tail began to flick. I knew exactly what she was thinking. What was Felinious doing giving away her secrets?

"It's true!" declared Felinious. "Furia's grandmother was the maker of your precious box."

Looking closely at the green wooden box, I saw that it looked very ancient indeed.

"The Antikittera?" laughed Periklaws, pointing at the box. "That cannot be! I don't have time for tall tales."

"Furia," said Felinous, "perhaps it might be helpful if you open up the box."

"Impossible!" snapped Periklaws. "The Antikittera has been sealed for centuries."

Furia's eyes flashed as she padded slowly over to the box. I followed her over to examine it.

"You will find that the first straybo fits neatly into the hole at the back of the box," explained Felinious. "It's a special kind of key."

Furia picked up the straybo and eased it into place. There was a solid click and the hinges of the box unlocked.

Periklaws gaped at the box in amazement. The guards stepped back.

"Impossible eh?" laughed Maxi. "Nothing's impossible for Furia."

The room fell silent for a while. Finally, Felinious spoke.

"What are you waiting for Furia? Open the box and see if your straybos will fit inside it."

Furia stepped towards the box.

"Wait child," cried Periklaws. "What was your grandmother's name?"

Furia turned towards him, her orange eyes blazing in the sunlight.

"Panpawra," she said, placing her paw lightly on the top of the ancient artefact.

Suddenly, Maxi let out a hiss of warning and dived headfirst at Furia with the beam in his paw. Furia span around in surprise.

"Don't open it!" cried Maxi. "For Peus sake Furia! Don't open that thing if you ever want to see the daylight again!"

Panpawra's Box

Maxi stood between Furia and the box. In his paw, he held the magic beam. His voice was serious.

"The legend says that Panpawra was given a box. The box contained all that is evil in the world: war; death; sickness; poverty; hunger. Panpawra was told never to open the box..."

Periklaws and the guards were staring at the box. I saw fear in their eyes. It was as if their precious relic had been transformed into a poisonous snake by Maxi's warning. Far below, the drums were beating for the games. Their dull heartbeat made Maxi's warning sound more serious.

"Furia," he ordered. "Step away from

that thing right now. Whatever you do, do not open the box. Something bad will happen. I know it!"

Felinious padded slowly towards Maxi with a kindly expression in his eyes.

"Maxipuss," he said. "You have hidden depths. Your knowledge of Squeak myths is impressive. But there are a couple of things that will set your heart at ease. According to the legend, Panpawra's box was not a square wooden box. It was a round jar made of stone. So this green wooden box cannot be the one in the legend."

Maxi stared at the beam in Felinious's paw. He didn't look convinced. His tail began to flick.

"How can we be sure?" asked Maxi.

'If I might borrow the beam for a moment..." he said, gently taking the magic beam from Maxi's paw. Before Maxi could react he held the beam up high in the air, next to the box."

"What do you see?" he boomed.

After a long pause, Periklaws spoke.

"Nothing," he said flatly.

"Periklaws is right," said Furia. "Where are the green sparks? Where is the magical light? The beam has no effect at all on this box."

Felinious nodded like an old teacher, pleased with his student's work.

Furia was right. The beam was dead wood in Felinious' paw.

"Correct Furia," Felinious said softly. "That's because this amazing box does not come from the mists and myths of Mount Olympuss." He paused and nodded at Periklaws. "This box belongs to the new world where knowledge has replaced magic. It was made by the paw of your grandmother."

Furia rested a paw on the lid of the box and took a deep breath.

"Wait!" cried Maxi. "Don't open it!"

The guards' paws went towards their swords. As I looked on, I felt a strange fear grip me. I had a terrible feeling that something bad was going to happen. My heart sunk as Furia slowly lifted the lid of the big green box. A beam of sunlight arrowed through the tent and lit up the golden insides of the wooden box. The gleaming contents dazzled our eyes.

"Treasure!" I gasped.

"Treasure indeed," said Felinious.

But when I looked closer, I saw that there were no gold bars or silver coins inside the box. It was full of clockwork workings: wheels and levers and dials gleaming brightly in the sunlight.

"Your straybos will fit nicely in there," said Felinious.

Furia unclipped the charms from her

collar and I saw that they were not really charms – but cogs and wheels – parts of the ancient mechanism of the Antikittera. Furia peered into the box, studying the clockwork machine.

"Thank Peus for that!" I gasped.

"Sorry," said Maxi. "I was wrong."

There was a slightly disappointed note in Maxi's voice. As if he'd wanted his warning about the box to be correct.

"Haven't you had enough magic this week?" I whispered. "Besides, if it really was Panpawra's box it would have been full of fleas."

Before Maxi could answer, there was a shout of triumph.

Periklaws gaped at the box in amazement. I heard the unmistakable sound of ticking.

"It's working!" cried Periklaws in amazement. "The Antikittera is working. We will hold a feast in your honour."

"Don't start celebrating yet," said Felinious, padding slowly to the box. He removed the straybos, took out the key and gave them back to Furia. Without saying another word to Periklaws, Felinious left the room and beckoned us to follow him.

The Antikittera

"Sit down," said Felinious. "This tale will take a while to tell."

When we were all sitting comfortably, he began.

"Furia's grandmother Panpawra had an amazing mind. She was a student of the great philosopher Herodicat himself. Her island was ruled by a king. The old king loved learning more than life itself. He collected knowledge from the far corners of the Feline Empire. He sat in his tall tower every night and gazed at the stars, trying to work out where the stars would move to next. It was important to know the positions of the stars so that we knew when to hold the Olympuss games. The king ordered Panpawra to create a machine for him – to put all this knowledge into a single box. He called this box *The Antikittera.*

The old king was not cruel. But he paid no attention to the lives of the poor islanders. He sat in his high tower with his books while they went hungry.

Then a new idea spread around the island. Like most great ideas, it came out of nowhere and spread faster than wildfire. The new idea was called 'democracy'. Instead of one king being in charge, everyone would vote on the island's laws. The old king was voted out by the cats of the island. They chased him away. The new leader of the island was a cat called Puris. But a group does not always make wise decisions. The islanders decided that the old king and all of his works were evil. They ruled that his box must be destroyed."

Felinious stared into the fire. Spirals of smoke curled and twisted as he went on with the story.

"Now Panpawra, (Furia's grandmother) had fallen in love and married a simple cat. He was not a scholar like his wife but he was curious about everything. He was good with money too. Can you guess the name of that cat?"

"Felinious," gasped Furia.

I drew my eyes from the fire and looked at Felinious in amazement.

"You mean... you are my grandfather," said an astonished Furia.

Felinious nodded.

For a moment I thought that Furia was going to leap up at him with a sword in her paw and start hissing like Mewdusa. But when I raised my eyes to look at her, I saw that there was no fire in her orange eyes."

"Grandfather?" she said in amazement. "But how...?"

Felinious shook his head sadly.

"I tried to persuade the islanders that they had nothing to fear but they refused to listen. They raged against Panpawra's machine. They made me throw it into the sea..."

"No!" cried Furia, leaping to her feet. The soft and warm hearted Furia had not lasted long.

"Wait my dear..." begged Felinious. "I have more to tell you."

Furia let out a hiss and finally sat down by the fire again.

"I'm sorry... But if I had not destroyed the machine – it would have been your grandmother and your mother who went over the cliff instead of that box."

"You saved their lives?" asked Furia.

"Yes," said Felinious. "But seeing her life's work destroyed was too much for your grandmother. It drove her mad. She never spoke another word to me."

Furia asked the question that had just popped into my mind.

"If you threw the box over the cliff, then what is this?" she said, pointing a paw at the Antikittera.

Felinious shook his head sadly.

"Your grandmother had been secretly working on a second box. A better version. It was finished when she died except for just four pieces."

A rage rose up within Felinious. Now his whisper had risen to an angry shout.

"Puris, the new leader, came to visit me. 'We've changed our minds, he said. Knowledge is important. We've heard about the second Antikittera box. We want to buy it, name your price.'"

As Furia looked seriously at Felinious, I saw that the familiar orange flash was back in her eyes.

"And you SOLD it?" she hissed.

"I was young," said Felinious. "Money is important to the young..."

Furia shook her head in disgust.

"How could you sell grandmother's memory like that?"

Felinious smiled.

"I sold the box, 'as seen'," said Felinious with a gleam in his eye. "But the buyers soon found that the Antikittera box did not work. There were four pieces missing."

Furia nodded, understanding breaking over her face in a warm wave.

"I decided to hide the missing pieces on my travels," said Felinious. "You call call them *straybos*. Periklaws has the box. But the four missing pieces belong to you my dear."

He held up the four straybos. "It is up to you to decide what to do with them."

We waited in silence for Furia to decide. At last she padded over to Felinious.

"So you are my grandfather?" she began.

"That's right my dear," said Felinious

"What kind of grandfather buys his own granddaughter at a slave market?"

Felinious let out a sigh.

"A determined one," he said. "I looked for you in your village. But the Romans had conquered. They'd taken you prisoner. It wasn't easy to track you down. We have Wulfren to thank for that."

Wulfren smiled. The old instructor had joined us in our tent. It was great to see him again but I knew this was not the time for a happy reunion.

Furia gave Felinious a hard look. Then her expression softened.

"Why didn't you explain about all this before?" she asked. "I hated it at your School for Strays."

Felinious looked a little hurt.

"You needed to be trained," he said.

"How do you know?" snapped Furia.

"Because if you had been trained properly, the Romans wouldn't have captured you in the first place," explained Felinious. "I knew that the quest to recover the straybos was going to be dangerous. I was young when I hid them. Young and impulsive. I travelled far and wide with the Roman army. I hid the straybos in out of the way places."

"Like the Maze of the Minopaw and a forbidden temple at the top of Mount Olympuss," I said.

No one took any notice of me.

"But I hated you and your school. I ran away three times!" said Furia.

"All part of the training," said

Felinious. Wulfren nodded.

"What now?" asked Maxi. "I guess we should all pack up and catch the next boat back to Rome."

"No," said Felinious. "Furia must decide what she wants from Periklaws. She can name her price. I if know Periklaws, he will pay anything in order to get the Antikittera box working again."

Furia looked at Felinious with a puzzled look on her face. You could tell that he was thinking about money, treasures beyond price and all of that.

"If you like my dear, I can negotiate for you," said Felinious with a gleam in his eye.

"He'll pay anything?" asked Furia.

"Anything!" said Felinious.

* *

"Thank you again Furia," I said as Maxi strapped on the boxing gloves.

"You two can thank me by winning your matches," said Furia with a smile.

Felinious wasn't pleased with his granddaughter's decision. Rather than asking for a ship load of gold and treasures, she'd only asked for one thing. Well, actually two things. The Olympuss games was buzzing with the talk of it. Periklaws had let Maxi and I take part in the games, even though we'd missed the official deadline. It hadn't been easy to get the proud Periklaws to break his precious rules for us. But he wanted the Antikittera machine to be complete again. So the deal was done and Maxi and I had a pass to the semi finals of the boxing. I was up first.

"So who are we up against?" asked Maxi.

"Not each other," I laughed. "Felinious thought that they might try that so he made sure it did not happen."

"So who am I fighting?" I asked.

"Hang on Spartan," said Maxi. "I'm looking, it's down here somewhere."

Maxi scanned down the list until he saw my name.

"You're up against... Demawtrius," he said. "Hey Spartan? Does that name sound familiar?"

"Demawtrius," growled Wulfren.

"I know him! He's the white cat who went for Maxi at the gate," I hissed.

The big Purrmanian nodded.

"It won't be easy," he said. "I've been watching him in action. He's already knocked out the champion."

My Big Match

I shouldn't have felt afraid. Yesterday, I'd faced down the deadly dog Furrburus, escaped from the monstrous Mewdusa and defeated an army of skeleton warriors. But that was yesterday. Today I was up against a white mountain of fur called Demawtrius. He was the very same son of Periklaws who had attacked Maxi at the gate. He'd hated getting a telling off. By the look of it he still had a chip on his shoulder the size of Mount Olympuss.

The crowd roared as Demawtrius stalked into the arena and glared. I got the feeling that Demawtrius wasn't particularly popular, but like any crowd, here at the Olympuss games they like to get behind the local cat.

I greeted Demawtrius with the traditional salute of the games.

"May the stars of Olympuss shine upon you," I said sportingly.

Demawtrius smashed one massive paw into the other, trying out his boxing gloves. He had paws like axe blades.

"I hate Romans," he hissed.

"I'm not a Roman," I replied.

"I hate gingers too," he growled.

It wasn't the first time I'd heard this insult. I expect that Demawtrius was the kind of fighter who fought best when he was angry. As I glared back at Demawtrius, I knew this wasn't going to be easy. I tried to remember the advice that Wulfren had given me in training.

"The smallest cat is always at a disadvantage," he'd told me.

"Thanks!" I thought to myself. I racked my brain but I couldn't remember anything useful. For Peus sake! Wulfren must have said something helpful... Then I remembered.

"It's all about speed and angles. Don't stand within their reach. Stay just outside their reach and make them miss you. Then, when they make a mistake, it'll be your turn to strike."

Demawtrius let out a low hiss. The crowd booed and jeered. The time for circling was over, it was time for the fight to begin. Demawtrius raised a paw and rushed towards me. The crowd roared. I side-stepped and danced away from him. He didn't seem particularly fast on his paws. I tried moving in and jabbing at his face but my blows didn't connect. Then I lost my balance. There was a crash like a hammer on my skull and a searing pain shot through my head.

"Miaoowch!!" I moaned. "That hurt!"

Why hadn't I entered the tree climbing?

I spat out a mouthful of dust but luckily I still had all of my teeth. I looked up at the mountain of fur in front of me. He was gloating. He waved at the crowd. Wulfren had warned me not to square up to him, but I couldn't resist it. Springing up, I let out a hiss and attacked with a left – right – left combination.

"Come on!" I cried, trying to get the crowd behind me as I darted in for another attack. Left – right – left. Boom!

Now the big bully Demawtrius was going to get a taste of his own medicine. Now the fur was going to start flying.

But when the fur started flying, it was ginger rather than white. I fired off blow after blow but most of them missed. The ones that didn't miss got blocked. In frustation, I moved in. I ducked down and then caught him square on the nose with my best shot. I waited for him to fall like a felled tree. But he didn't crash to the ground. He just stood there laughing.

"Is that all you've got?" he hissed. I stepped to the left to dodge the next blow but he was too fast. His punch crashed through my defences. I felt a blinding stab of pain. Then everything went black. It was as if someone had covered up my eyes with a blanket.

"Demawtrius is the winner!" I heard the commentator say. The stars of Olympuss flashed before my eyes. Then it all went black.

Pawscript

When I woke up my head was clanging like a hammer factory. I put my paw to my jaw and winced.

The first voice I heard was Maxi's.

"Nice to have you back Spartan," he laughed. "We were worried about you."

"What happened?" I moaned.

"You lost by a knockout," he said. "They had to carry you out of the arena."

I let out a groan.

"But the good news is, I took revenge for you," he said. "I defeated Demawtrius in the final."

"Really?" I gasped. "You knocked out that white wind-bag?"

"I won on points," laughed Maxi. "But I knocked the smile of his face. You should have seen the look on his face when they gave me the prize."

I lay still in silence thinking about what had happened. Maxi was the champion of Olympuss. I was the king of the losers.

"Come on Spartan," said Maxi. "There

are not many cats that could stand up to a beast like Demawtrius. Wulfren said you fought like a lion."

I waited for the punchline but there was none. For once, Maxi was serious.

"Even Furia said she was impressed with your courage," he continued.

"Really?" I said.

"Really!" said a familiar voice.

When I looked up, I saw Furia standing over my bed.

"There was no need to prove your courage in the ring Son of Spartapuss," she said. "You've proved that ten times already on this adventure."

Furia looked at me. Her orange eyes were shining. Perhaps there was a lot she wanted to say. But she was a cat of so few words. The look on her face was enough.

"I'm afraid I don't remember much about what happened since we left *The Pawgo*," I said. That whack on my head must have wiped my memory.

Maxi told the whole story. It took a

long time to tell. How we'd looked for Furia and the trouble with the beam, and Furrburus. Then the skeleton warriors and the battle with Mewdusa. By the time he'd finished explaining about Panpawra's box, my head was hurting.

"There's still one thing that's bothering me." I said.

"What's that Spartan?" asked Maxi. "Is it the 'hope' thing? That's easy. When all of the bad stuff flew out of Panpawra's box then there was nothing left inside. It was empty. Only hope remained. So the story is saying that we should never give up hope Spartan. Get it?"

Maxi looked pleased with himself after explaining this.

"I get that," I sighed. "But something is still bothering me."

"What?" he asked. I scratched my chin, took a deep breath and began.

"Panpawra's box had all the evil things in the world in it – right?"

"Right," said Maxi.

"And Peus didn't want anyone to open

it in case all the bad stuff came out?"

"Right again," nodded Maxi. "So why in the name of flaming Furrburus did Peus give her the box in the first place, if he didn't want her to open it?!" I asked.

Maxi sat quietly for a moment and his tail began to flick. He scratched his ear, got up, circled twice and sat down again. For the first time since I'd met him, Maxi was completely lost for words. He thought and thought, but he didn't have an answer.

"All right," he moaned. "I admit it. You've really got me there Son of Spartapuss! You've defeated me at last."

The Olympuss Games Series

BOOK I Son of Spartapuss   ISBN: 9781906132811
BOOK II Eye of the Cyclaw   ISBN: 9781906132835
BOOK III Maze of the Minopaw ISBN: 9781906132828
BOOK IV Stars of Olympuss   ISBN: 9781906132842

www.mogzilla.co.uk/shop

I AM SPARTAPUSS

Rome AD 36. The mighty Feline Empire rules the world. Spartapuss, a ginger cat is comfortable managing Rome's finest Bath and Spa. But Fortune has other plans for him. Spartapuss is arrested and imprisoned by Catligula, the Emperor's heir. Sent to a school for gladiators, he must fight and win his freedom in the Arena - before his opponents make dog food out of him.

'This witty Roman romp is history with cattitude.' Junior Magazine (Scholastic)

ISBN: 978-1-906132-42-2

www.spartapuss.co.uk